# Hugs

## Robert Munsch

**illustrated by**
## Michael Martchenko

Scholastic Canada Ltd.
Toronto  New York  London  Auckland  Sydney
Mexico City  New Delhi  Hong Kong  Buenos Aires

Scholastic Canada Ltd.
604 King Street West, Toronto, Ontario M5V 1E1, Canada

Scholastic Inc.
557 Broadway, New York, NY 10012, USA

Scholastic Australia Pty Limited
PO Box 579, Gosford, NSW 2250, Australia

Scholastic New Zealand Limited
Private Bag 94407, Botany, Manukau 2163, New Zealand

Scholastic Children's Books
Euston House, 24 Eversholt Street, London NW1 1DB, UK

www.scholastic.ca

The illustrations in this book were painted in watercolour
on Crescent illustration board.
The type is set in 22 point Berkeley.

Library and Archives Canada Cataloguing in Publication

Munsch, Robert N., 1945-, author
Hugs / Robert Munsch ; illustrated by Michael Martchenko.

Originally published: Toronto : Scholastic Canada Ltd., ©2014.
ISBN 978-1-4431-4290-8 (pbk.)

I. Martchenko, Michael, illustrator  II. Title.

PS8576.U575H85 2015          jC813'.54          C2014-905964-7

6 5 4 3 2 1          Printed in Malaysia  108          15 16 17 18 19

*For Thea and Tate Hedemann*
*Saskatoon, Saskatchewan.*
                                    — R.M.

The day that Thea was
mad at Mommy, she took her
little brother Tate's hand and
walked out the front door.

After they had walked for a long time, Tate said, "I need a hug."

So Thea gave him a hug.

"That was not the right kind of hug," said Tate. "Try something different."

"Right!" said Thea. "Something different!"

So they walked and walked and walked and finally came to a huge snail.

"How about a hug for my little brother?" said Thea.

"Hug?" said the snail. "I love to give hugs."

And the snail gave Tate a big snail hug.

"How was that?" said Thea.

"Slime! Slime! Lots of slime! Yuck!" yelled Tate.

"OK!" said Thea. "Not a good hug."

Then they walked and walked
and walked and finally came to a
huge skunk.

"How about a hug for my little
brother?" said Thea.

"Hug?" said the skunk. "I love
to give hugs."

And the skunk gave Tate a big
skunk hug.

"How was that?" said Thea.

"Stink! Stink! Very yucky stink!" yelled Tate.

"OK!" said Thea. "Not a good hug."

Then they walked and walked and walked and finally came to a huge porcupine.

"How about a hug for my
little brother?" said Thea.
"Hug?" said the porcupine.
"I love to give hugs."

And the porcupine gave Tate a big porcupine hug.

"How was that?" said Thea.

"Needles! Needles! Sharp poky needles!" yelled Tate.

"OK!" said Thea. "Not a good hug."

Then they walked and walked and walked and finally came to a huge gorilla.

"How about a hug for my little brother?" said Thea.

"Hug?" said the gorilla. "I love to give hugs."

And the gorilla gave Tate a big gorilla hug.

"How was that?" said Thea.

"Hard! Hard! Much too hard!" yelled Tate.

So Thea took her little brother's hand and they walked all the way back home.

Mommy said, "How was your walk?"

"Tate got hugged by a snail," said Thea.

"Slime! Slime! Lots of slime!" yelled Tate.

"And Tate got hugged by a skunk," said Thea.

"Stink! Stink! Very yucky stink!" yelled Tate.

"And Tate got hugged by a porcupine," said Thea.

"Needles! Needles! Sharp poky needles!" yelled Tate.

"And Tate got hugged by a gorilla," said Thea.

"Hard! Hard! Much too hard!" yelled Tate. "I need a Mommy hug."

So Mommy gave Tate a Mommy hug and Tate said, "Just right, just right, a just right hug."

"And the Thea who walked out the door so mad," said Mommy, "who hugged her?"

"Nobody," said Thea. "Nobody gave me a hug, and I am waiting for a Mommy hug."

So Mommy hugged Thea and Thea said, "Just right, just right, a just right hug."

And then they all had lunch.